AF254602

Gypsy's Wedding

And other
Short
Tales

By Darby Patterson

Bolton Road
PUBLISHING

*For all the unsuspecting people who allowed me to
peek (undetected) inside their lives and
without ever knowing it,
created these short stories.*

Full Disclosure: Every story in this little collection is based on a real encounter with real people who had no idea they were being observed and recorded in the memory of a journalist trained to take note of small details.

I have, because imagining is great fun, embellished their stories, except in the case of the piece that closes the book, which is driven by characters who needed no exaggeration. I appear in this story and publicly admit to witnessing the comedic tragedy decades ago.

CONTENTS

Gypsy's Wedding   1

Crossing the Channel   47

The Attic   54

A New Year on the Rails   77

The Conversation   84

The Morning Watch   91

When a Home is Not   94

1.
Gypsy's Wedding

Gypsy Latreaux peered into the smoky bathroom mirror. This time she'd get it right, finally.

She poked a last carnation into her upswept hair that made her neck look long and graceful. There was no hint of lines or sagging skin that often afflicted women her age. The white flowers encircled her curls like a crown of petals and also camouflaged the army of bobby pins that held up her hairdo.

Her dress was pewter blue with a waistline cinched in by satin ribbon laces of the same color.

Damn, she wished that Bubba had a full-length mirror in his doublewide. She'd have to wait till they got to the courthouse to check out the whole picture. But, she already knew she was looking good, and Bubba was damn lucky to have her. Here she was, somewhere in her early 40s with the tiny waistline of a 15-year-old. She didn't have all that many wrinkles and her teeth weren't too bad, considering.

She draped a powder blue, gauze floor-length cape over her shoulders - from head to toe looking like a mature, southern version of the Princess Bride. A Loretta Lynn tune floating through her brain as she sashayed from the bathroom down the narrow hallway that emptied into the compact living room.

Bubba reclined in a Barcalounger watching ESPN on the 36-inch flatscreen, Lone Star Beer in one hand and a Camel in the other. Gypsy posed in the doorway. "Well, what'd ya think?"

"I think them sumabitches gonna lose again," he answered, keeping his eyes glued to the screen.

"No, Bubba, baby – I mean what'dya think of me. Do I look like a bride?" Bubba rotated his head 45 degrees and checked her out.

"I'll say. You clean up real good. I am one lucky cuss. Shee-itt!" His attention snapped back to the screen where the Cowboy's defensive end had just racked up a penalty. Undaunted and carrying on the princess theme Gypsy said, "Thank you kind sir." She smiled sweetly. "We better think about getting on over to the courthouse, Bubba. I sure want to be there when Patsy Mae Wilson comes flyin' in."

"Five minutes, baby. It's the last of the fourth. They could still pull it off."

Gypsy sighed and lit a cigarette. She wasn't about to have an argument on the most important day of her life. Of course, there had been a few other similar "important days," but she'd have been a fool to stay with an unemployed carpenter who liked to wear her pantyhose or that bozo with the alligators. Bubba was all right. Had a steady job. Owned the mobile home outright. Drove a nice quarter-ton F150 and had a motorcycle to boot.

She looked at her husband to be. Big man. Tall, well over six feet. He had that wild, natural sort of look you find in men who prefer a rural environment. His graying hair tickled the collar of the black western dress shirt he wore under a black denim vest. Gypsy didn't mind the longish hair, but she didn't much care for the beard. At least Bubba could trim it now and then. Jesus, he looked like Father Time. But she kept her silence, figuring that was something she could fix after they were man and wife. Along with that beer belly of his. The man could pass for eight months along!

On the drive into Austin, Gypsy sidled up next to Bubba and put her hand on his leg. She moved it softly up and down the stiff black denim, knowing that if she wanted to, she could drive Bubba right out of his mind. Lust played a pretty big part in their attraction for each other, and it was a lot more fun than talking. To pass the time, Gypsy sang "Your Cheatin' Heart" and noticed that it had brought a little smile to Bubba's lips. She had some worry about his mood because the Cowboys did not, in fact, pull it off. Bubba had the potential to be righteously crabby.

They were getting married in the city because her very best friend from elementary school was flying all the way in from Australia to be her bride's maid, and there wasn't any airport back there in Austin's Hill Country. Gypsy had looked at a map to find out precisely where Australia was. It was a hell of a long way off and an island to boot. Bubba told her that everybody in Australia was a criminal except for the "Originals" who were cannibals. Gypsy didn't believe him because Patsy Mae wasn't a crook, and neither was the man she went over there to marry. He was a rancher with plenty of money and land.

A handful of other friends were meeting them at the courthouse as well. The crowd was limited by the number of running vehicles in their circle of acquaintances. No matter, pretty soon Gypsy would be a Mrs. for the best and final time. Gypsy checked herself out in the rearview mirror. Some of the carnations were looking a little droopy.

They drove into the city with its tall glass and steel buildings and saw the Goddess of Liberty atop the great dome of the capitol building. Winding through construction and one-way streets they pulled up in front of the courthouse. "You got any quarters?" Bubba asked her. Gypsy said she only had the tens and twenties she was saving for the celebration after.

"I get a dang ticket, it's your fault," Bubba said. He jumped out of the cab and stood on the sidewalk, hoisting up his jeans.

"Aren't you forgetting something?" Gypsy asked and extended her hand. "You going to help your future wife from this here carriage like a gentleman?"

Bubba reached out to her, and she slid down off the seat on the driver's side. It was a brilliant winter afternoon, cool air kissed by the sun. She slid her arm into Bubba's and gave him her best smile. "The Lord has smiled upon this day," she said. "Couldn't be finer weather for getting' married."

"That's so," Bubba responded. "But while he was at it, He might've smiled on them Cowboys. I lost ten damn bucks."

They walked toward the courthouse doors, big carved wooden doors that looked too heavy to open by hand. Gypsy carried two small bouquets of carnations in her hand, one for herself and the other for her bridesmaid.

The hometown members of the wedding party had already arrived and were waiting at the bottom of the steps, smoking cigarettes and grinning at the couple walking toward them. Except for Gypsy, the color of the day appeared to be black, though no one had sent out any memos about dress. The Preacher, Bubba's best friend, and frequent designated driver, pulled himself up to his full five-foot-four height. He was wearing his best hat – a black Stetson with a silver-conch band holding a hawk's feather. The rest of his outfit was standard black-on-black - shirt, vest, jeans, boots with pointy toes. He'd trimmed his white beard for the occasion and given his handlebar mustache an extra turn on the ends. Bright blue eyes peeked out from beneath the brim of the Stetson.

Towering over him at six-foot-two and shoulders wide as the midsection of a whiskey barrel, Billy Ray wore a grin of genuine joy and anticipation. His lips parted some, revealing the absence of two incisors and a couple of lower teeth. He was honoring the occasion by wearing his black sports coat with the narrow blue stripe and dress pants that very nearly matched. His black T-shirt had been freshly laundered by his mama, who looked after him and had stuffed a white hanky in the breast pocket of the sports coat. The jacket was covering up a cute drawing of a squirrel on the front of the T-shirt. Lettering on the back read, "Squirrel, It's Not Just for Breakfast Anymore."

Bubba and Billy's mama had been real good friends, and Bubba tended to treat the slow but well-intentioned young man like a son. In his beefy hands, Billy grasped a bouquet of yellow daisies that he had squeezed till the stems turned to limp green strings.

Between the two men was a short, stout woman with lemon blond hair and strawberry-red lips. Stella Curry had once been the toast of the Hill Country among gentleman of a certain social circle that frequented the Blue Dawg – a homey late-night spot just off Highway 87 near Brady. Though it had been many years ago, Stella assiduously hung onto her former glamour and was thus sporting one of her better gowns – the black cocktail dress with sequins on the bodice and a layer of flamingo pink gathers around the hemline. It had been quite a trick to fit into the dress that morning, and she'd required help from two people to urge the zipper up as she sucked in her belly and held her breath. One of her friends had made an unwelcome joke about stuffing sausage as they collaborated on the effort.

Stella had also applied black false eyelashes and an extra layer of pancake makeup and rouge, thinking that she just might find somebody interesting later at the reception. But she was already counting the minutes to when the zipper would come down and release her innards to fully suck in air. Stella was picking at her teased hairdo with a pointy comb, hoping to conceal the dark roots that had sprouted in the depths of the blond mound.

The Preacher spoke as Bubba and Gypsy reached them. "Well, look at you two! Like the cover of a magazine. Lord be praised. He has looked down upon you." He reached out his hand and shook Bubba's, grasping Bubba's elbow with the other in a sign of a deeper kind of friendship. "This is the Big Day."

The Preacher turned his eyes on Gypsy and said the words she longed to hear from Bubba. "And you Missy Bride, pretty as a picture and twice as fine." Gypsy started to lift the sides of her dress to curtsy, but the Preacher had grabbed her around the waist and was giving her a close up hug in which the lower regions of their bodies briefly, but firmly, met.

It was back-slapping and hugs all around, except for Billy Ray, who was never quite certain what was appropriate in social situations. Stella craned her neck up and looked at the big boy. "Billy Ray, what you planning to do with them flowers? Plant em,'?" she asked. "Give them flowers to Ms. Gypsy here."

Suddenly aware of the bouquet and the long stems surrendering to his grip, he reached out his arm and handed them to the bride. "Here, Ms. Gypsy. These are from me and my mama. She said to send you her good luck wishes." Billy Ray's smiled widened, giving him the appearance of an oblong jack-o-lantern. Gypsy graciously accepted the flowers and handled the situation of the drooping stems. She broke off the blossoms and stuffed a couple of daisies into the lapel-holes of the men's jackets. She poked Stella's behind the woman's left ear, penetrating numerous layers of hairspray to position it correctly. She saved the rest for herself and for her bridesmaid, Patsy Mae.

Just then, a black Lincoln Towne Car pulled up to the curb. "That just might be Patsy Mae," Gypsy said. "You know her husband owns a big old ranch, and I'll bet he has a garage full of cars like that."

"You s'pose them cars have paddlewheels on 'em?" Bubba joked. "Cuz I done told you that Australia is a dang island!" Gypsy smacked him in the belly with the back of her hand.

"Course I know that! I'm just sayin' that Patsy Mae's done all right by herself. Anyway, it ain't her."

A black driver in a suit and livery cap had opened the rear door for a paunchy, older white man who was having some trouble rising from the car seat. He gripped the sides of the door and pulled himself out, waving away the assistance offered by his driver. Judge Herman Floutz was fresh from the golf course and wearing a jaunty little cap that pushed his white hair out like bat wings alongside his ruddy face. His double chin flapped from side to side as he righted himself. The judge moved his bulk down the sidewalk heading for the wedding party as the driver stood at attention beside the sleek car.

He walked slowly, with a broken gait as if he was experiencing some pain, although the main impediment was the fact that the Judge was still wearing his spiked golf shoes and was at least 100 pounds overweight. The Judge had told his secretary to call him on his mobile precisely a half-hour before the wedding and well into the Saturday round of golf that he was guaranteed to lose, along with a hefty wager. The phone peeled just as the Judge lopped a divot the size of Rhode Island onto the fairway, his ball heading for a sand trap. Bailing on the 11th hole after the call, the

Judge said, "Hell's Bells, ya'll have to play ahead without me. Dang secretary double-booked me. Sorry as I can be. And just when I felt my game taking a turn. Y 'all have a drink from the cart on me." He made this offer knowing the $15 for beer would be considerably less than the bet he'd made on the outcome of the game.

Judge Floutz stopped in front of the wedding party and lifted his head, eyeballing his customers. "Stella," he said letting a lurid grin swipe across his face and nodding a greeting. "Billy Ray, Preacher, Bubba. Good to see ya'll under *other* circumstances." Billy Ray was very impressed with the Judge's friendliness, having experienced his Honor's wrath after the incident with the blue pig. Bubba and the Preacher felt a mite pissed off by the remark, but held their tongues.

Stella looked the judge up and down. "My sentiments exactly, Judge Floutz, ya'll know what I mean?" The Judge snorted. There was a knowing smile on Stella's lips, and a shade of purple-red crawled up the jurist's neck.

Although she wasn't certain about the details, Gypsy knew something negative was inappropriately brewing on her wedding day. "Judge, let me introduce myself," she said, extending her hand in greeting. "I am Gypsy Latreaux, the bride-to-be, and I am pleased to make your acquaintance."

The Judge shook her hand and gifted her with the kind of smile he only used on the campaign trail. "Well, the pleasure is mine, ma'am. And may I inquire about your origins? I don't believe I've seen you before in our fair city, whereas I am acquainted with your colleagues."

"I hail from the fine city of N'awlins, your honor," Gypsy said, batting her eyes.

"Gypsy here is a entertainer," Stella offered.

"I see," said the judge raising one eyebrow.

"She sings," Bubba interjected, guessing the direction the Judge's imagination was headed.

"Well now, that's real nice. Would I have had the pleasure of hearing any of your recordings?" the Judge asked politely, trying to keep Stella from participating in the conversation.

"I mostly sing at fairs and little clubs," Gypsy said, "although I did have a gentleman promise me a recording contract once. Turned out he was married." Gypsy shook her head and shrugged her shoulders.

"Aren't they all?" added Stella, looking at the Judge.

"Yes, well," the judge cleared a bullfrog from his throat. "Looks like you might have done right by yourself this time. To my knowledge, your groom here is not in a marital state." To Bubba he said, "Talented little lady you got for yourself."

"Regular songbird," Bubba offered. Gypsy wasn't sure just how Bubba meant this. She had been longing for him to pay attention to her singing, say something complimentary. On the other hand, she seemed to recall that "songbird" had a sort of negative connotation. And Bubba had used the tone of voice that he sometimes used to say the opposite of what he really meant. "Put that thought clean out of your mind Miss Gypsy," she thought to herself. "Negative, negative!"

On balance, Bubba was not a bad deal. There came a time in every woman's life when priorities shifted. So Bubba was not the youngest, best-looking guy on the planet. In fact, he was a genuine slob of a man. So, he might not fully appreciate her God-given vocal talents that could have landed her in Nashville had she done a few things differently a decade or two ago. For example, the clogging gig with the carnival out of Sarasota was probably not a good career move.

But, the man had a house on a semi-permanent foundation, running transportation, a source of income, and he wasn't all that bad in bed.

The judge slowly climbed the stairs. "See y'all in my chambers," he grunted. His golf shoes left little peas of dirt on the marbled steps. "We'll be there shortly," Gypsy trilled. "We're just waiting on my best friend. She's coming all the way from Australia for my wedding. She is a wealthy woman!"

As if on cue, a taxi pulled up to the curb and, without waiting for the driver to open the door, a red-headed woman with a tan that was incongruous to her hair color, burst out and ran down the sidewalk into Gypsy's waiting arms. The women embraced like teenage girls, squealing and jumping in circles like a pair of Spanish dancers. The wedding party stood grinning, waiting. Finally, the reunited friends held each other at arm's length to assess the passage of time. Gypsy quickly noticed the landscape of fine lines that were etched on Patsy Mae's face, kind of like the pattern on a shattered windshield.

"You are lookin' fine! Not a day over 21!" She said to Patsy.

"You lie as good as ever," Patsy said. "That sun Down Under just dries your face up like an old prune! But you, Gypsy Latreaux, you look like a young bride. Like a Princess Bride in that dress."

Gypsy noticed that Patsy Mae's dress was a little crumpled from travel and that she was wearing casual sandals, no doubt for comfort through the long trip. The real sign of her friend's good destiny was right there on her ring finger. Gypsy held Patsy's hand out and was almost blinded by three of the biggest diamonds she'd ever seen. Bubba had promised to get her a real wedding ring down the road. For now, she settled for his sterling silver Harley ring. Gypsy turned to the wedding party and made enthusiastic introductions.

"This is Clyde Rumsfield, Patsy, but folks around here call him Preacher – cause, well, he has a very spiritual way of talking." She tried to explain Billy Ray's presence, but since she didn't entirely understand it herself, just called him a young friend of Bubba's. Stella stepped up and introduced herself. "I take care of everybody around here, honey," she said. "There is nothing that happens in this town or in those hills yonder that I don't know about."

"I am just so please to meet you all," Patsy Mae said, spreading her smile across the wedding party. "As we say back home, G'day!"

"Listen to her talk Australian," Gypsy chirped just as three loud blasts sounded from the taxi. "Criminy, I was so excited to see you, Gypsy, I forgot to pay the cab driver," Patsy Mae started to rifle through her bulging purse. "Now, what did I do with my wallet? Hello, hello, where are you?" she sang to the seemingly bottomless bag. The horn blasted again and a head wearing a white turban emerged over the roof of the taxi. The driver stared keenly at Patsy Mae.

"Twenty dollas!" he shouted.

"Oh, bugger! I think my wallet is in my suitcase," Patsy said.

Enchanted with what she took to be 'Australian,' Gypsy pulled a twenty out of the bodice of her wedding dress. "Here honey, you can pay me back later."

"You are just a doll, as always," Patsy Mae trilled and ran back toward the cab. She returned, pulling a large, worn suitcase that bounced and rolled behind her. Gypsy recalled that her friend had been quite a dresser, so the fact that she seemed to have packed for a month instead of a long weekend was not surprising. She told Bubba to toss the bulging suitcase in the back of the pickup.

"Sure. Billy Ray, why doncha just heave that bag into the truck bed," Bubba ordered. There was nothing Billy liked more than being helpful and a smile lit up his face. By all accounts, including his own, Billy was not real smart, but he compensated by being helpful to folks and being strong as a Clydesdale in heat. This was both a blessing and a curse as Billy didn't have a firm grasp on when to use his God-given muscles. It was this proclivity that had landed him in front of Judge Floutz more than once. But since Bubba had never asked him to do anything that got him either a whuppin' from his mom or trouble with the law, Billy was happy to sling the big suitcase like it was full of empty beer cans instead of Patsy's wardrobe.

"Well, just look at that!" Patsy warbled. "Aren't you the strong one? Thank you kindly." She returned

Billy's smile - the difference being the number and condition of teeth they showed to each other.

"Tell the lady 'you're welcome," Bubba instructed.

"You're welcome," Billy Ray said, lowering his eyes and shifting from one foot to the other. Gypsy was once again congratulating herself for choosing such a gentleman this time around. She looked dreamily up at Bubba. "Shall we?" she asked, raising her eyebrows alluringly.

"Right here, in front of God and everybody?" Bubba smirked. Gypsy hauled off and belted him in the bicep, causing Bubba to laugh heartily at the off-color joke he'd made and making Billy take a protective step forward in case he was needed to defend Bubba from further attack.

Gypsy linked arms with her betrothed, and the wedding party moved through the ornate courthouse doors with the kind of awe befitting the gates of Oz. Being the weekend, the hallway was nearly empty, and the stone floors were buffed to a high shine. Dark wood wainscoting decorated the bottom portion of the walls and above hung larger-than-life portraits of long

-dead, stern-faced white men whose eyes appeared to follow the gaggle of people below. Gold picture lights illuminated the portraits. "I wonder who all these folks were?" Gypsy whispered. So elegant and hallowed was the courthouse that it seemed church-like behavior was called for.

Patsy Mae glanced up at a man in a blue uniform with a gold sash across his chest. "Rich, that's what they were," she said. The group walked slowly along the corridor, the heels of Gypsy's shoes tapping sharp echoes. Patsy's sandals flapped against her bare heels.

"Why y'all whisperin'?" Stella blurted out. "This ain't the dang Cathedral of the Bleedin' Heart. It's Floutz's office!"

"It just has that feel about it," Gypsy answered. "I have never been here before." She stopped in her tracks. "I'll bet my songs would sound dang good in this hallway!"

"Go ahead, honey," Stella barked. "Light one up!"

Thus, as they proceeded slowly to the mahogany double doors of the judge's chambers, Gypsy served up a taste of "Amazing Grace" that floated on the air and bounced off the high ceiling and ricocheted off the walls and floor. She sounded like a throaty choir of fallen angels singing for sweet redemption.

At the courtroom doors, they paused. "Was blind but now I seeeeeeeeee," Gypsy crooned, liberally decorating the notes of the last two words. Then silence fell like a velvet curtain. The party stood immobilized until Bubba reached out and grasped the over-sized brass doorknob. The heavy door swung slowly open, letting out a stream of cool air. They moved forward, feet falling on a red and gold carpet that repeated the ornamentation of wood carving on long benches that stretched clear up to the bar separating magistrate from the masses.

Gypsy and Bubba led the way. The Preacher, Stella and Patsy followed close behind. Billy was absent. "Where'd that boy go?" Bubba asked and marched to the back of the courtroom. He opened the door to find Billy immobilized like a freeze-dried flounder. "What's wrong with you Billy Ray? Come on. We're waiting on you," Bubba said.

"I cain't go in there, Bubba. I cain't go back to that jail. It wasn't my fault!"

"What are you talkin' about. This here is my wedding. I'm getting hitched. You ain't in trouble Billy Ray."

"You promise? You'll tell that judge?"

"Just git your butt inside this here room. I think that judge charges by the minute!" Bubba held the door open, and Billy Ray walked in like a frightened kindergartener on the first day of school.

"I didn't do it, Bubba," Billy quickly whispered. "It wasn't really me who painted the pig."

"It don't matter Billy. This here has nothing to do with that. Just take a seat and be quiet. You think you can do that for me?"

"Yessir."

"And take off your cap. It ain't respectful."

"Yessir." He slid the cap, emblazoned with a Hooters logo, into his back pocket and sat down beside the preacher.

Stella readjusted her chest inside the suffocating dress. "Old Floutz likes to keep people waiting. Makes him feel important," she said in a low voice. "He's probably back there in those chambers of his practicing his putting."

"How come you know him so good?" Gypsy asked.

"We go back a long way, honey. Someday, I tell you all about it. But this ain't the time or the place."

An enormous elevated judge's bench dominated the courtroom. A rich smooth, deep brown, it showed graceful wood grain that swirled like smoke across its surface. The Preacher was in awe. "Looks like an altar, that does," he said. "High justice from on high."

As if trying to prove Stella wrong, Judge Floutz came bursting in from a door that was stage right to the courtroom. From the sleeve of his black flowing robe, the Judge pulled a white handkerchief and first blew his nose and then wiped his brow. ""Bout hot enough to make a sidewinder go straight," he said, walking in front of the dais." "Gather round now. Come on. Don't be shy. You too, Billy. I ain't gonna bite."

Stella let out a snort, and the Judge shot a glance her way. "Bubba, you and Miss Latreaux stand right in front of me. The rest of you file in behind them so I don't have to shout." The party moved into place, and Gypsy grabbed Patsy Mae by the hand, pulled her to her side and handed her a bouquet. "You're my brides-maid, honey. Get right in here."

"Now, Bubba, you got your choice of ceremonies. I can do the short kind or I can lengthen it out. What'll you have?"

"What's the difference?" Bubba asked

"Oh, about $50 or so," Judge Floutz answered.

"I think what Bubba was asking, your Honor," Gypsy said. "Is what is the difference in the ceremony?"

"I knew that! Well, the budget ceremony takes about five minutes and the other takes a good fifteen, cause I put in all the whereas'es and whyfore's and such. The brides, they seem to like that."

Gypsy looked into Bubba's eyes. "Well, I ain't like everybody," Gypsy said. "If we take the five-minute ceremony we can get over to Friday's in time for happy hour. They got a killer Juke Box. I'd rather spend the money on that."

"That's my girl," Bubba said with a smile. "Practical."

"Okay, let's get started," the Judge ordered, and everyone straightened up like cadets awaiting inspection. The Judge momentarily closed his eyes and threw his head back, waiting for inspiration. His generous chins stretched out, making him appear frog-like. The silence continued. All eyes were on the judge who snapped-to as if he'd been jolted awake from a dream.

"Dang, I hate it when that happens!" he said and stormed up the stairs to his bench where he grabbed a big, green book with gold leaf pages. "Forgot how to start. Happens when you got a ton of things on your mind." He turned to somewhere in the middle of the book. "I got it marked." The judge took a sip from a blue plastic cup on his bench as he read a passage. "Aaahhh," he uttered.

Stella leaned over to Patsy Mae. "That ain't water in that cup," she whispered. "Take my word for it."

Floutz brought both the book and the cup with him when he returned to preside over the wedding. "Ya'll ready?" he asked as if it had been his clients holding things up.

"All right, let's get on with it." He looked back and forth from Bubba to Gypsy before tilting his head back again. "Dang, dang!"

"Dearly beloved," the Preacher spoke up, prompting the Judge.

"I knew that!" Floutz barked. "I was just setting the tone." He cleared his throat. "Dearly Beloved, we are gathered here to unite Bubba Smith and Gypsy Latreaux in holy matrimony." He stopped and looked quizzically at Bubba. "By the way, that your real name? I mean, I never did meet anyone with Bubba as a given name. It'd be illegal for me to marry this lil' lady to a nickname."

"My mama named me Bubba, Judge. It's smack on the birth certificate. Told me she wanted a name that was more uncommon than Smith."

"Just makin' sure. Stayin' within the guidelines of the court. Now, where was I?" The Judge looked up at the ornate ceiling.

" ... unite Bubba Smith and Gypsy Latreaux in holy matrimony," the Preacher said. "Now comes the part about ..."

"I am going to hold you in contempt of court if there's another outburst Mr. Rumsfield."

"My apologies, your Honor. Just tryin' to help," the Preacher said.

"Well, it's throwin' my game off," the judge said, sticking his lower lip out like a pouting six-year-old. "Here, hold this for a minute." He handed Patsy Mae his blue cup and Gypsy the big legal book. He started slapping his body with his hands. "Glasses. Lookin' for my glasses. What did I do with those dang things?"

Stella rolled her eyes as the judge thwacked his robes some more. "On your head," Stella said, grinning and pointing to the Judge's shiny pate where the rimless pair of glasses rested. Billy suddenly grasped what had happened and struggled to hold in a laugh. A courtroom, he knew, was not a place to laugh. But the situation with the judge and the glasses and Stella was just too funny, and a laugh started escaping – first from his nose, sounding like a grunt, and then full out, punctuated with snorts.

"Order in the court!" the Judge commanded, and Billy held his breath. It was quiet as the Judge put the specs on his nose, took the book from Gypsy, and turned to the page with the 50 dollar ceremony. He took up where he had left off, reading the proper words to avoid any further unfortunate events. "Is there anyone present here who knows why this couple should not be united in matrimony? Speak now or forever hold your peace." Floutz looked up, fully expecting no response. But Billy had his hand raised.

"Billy? You have something to say?"

"I'm sorry." Billy said, hanging his head.

"I am just sorry. I didn't mean to, but I was holding my breath so hard I couldn't help it. I'm sorry Uncle Bubba."

"What are you talkin' about?" the Judge demanded. As the words slipped out, it became clear to everyone in the courtroom what Billy was apologizing for. A wafting odor had attached itself to the molecules in the air – a smell reminiscent of cabbage and baked beans.

Bubba turned. "Excuse yourself from the room, Billy. It's all right," he said quietly. "We'll see you outside. You wait." Bubba turned to the Judge. "I think you best get on with it." Billy turned and scuttled out of the courtroom.

The Judge was pressing the wadded up hanky to his face. Gypsy and Patsy buried their noses in the bouquets of carnations. Stella covered her face with her hands. The Preacher and Bubba pushed through the pain.

"UnderthepowervestedinmeInowpronounceyouma nandwife," the Judge garbled, reaching out and snatching his cup from Patsy's hand. "You might want to wait to kiss the bride outside. Court is adjourned."

Floutz bolted from the room with amazing speed, considering his physical condition. The wedding party also didn't tarry. They moved as one motivated body through the courtroom doors and into blessed air, where Billy was waiting on the steps.

He was red-faced and shifting from one foot to the next. He opened his mouth to apologize, but Bubba and his bride cut him off. "It's okay, Billy," Bubba said. "I get gas myself sometimes."

"Don't you fret," Gypsy added. "I'm just so dang happy, I could sing!"

Patsy Mae was teary-eyed. "It was so beautiful. If I had half a voice, I'd sing with you!"

"Let's all sing," Gypsy said. "What's a song we all know?"

It was Stella who started the rendition of "Don't Let Your Babies Grow Up to be Cowboys," that the wedding party sang in a chorus as they headed for the reception in the lounge at T.G.I. Friday's.

It was early evening, and the bar wasn't crowded. There was only Gypsy's party and a scattering of suited-up people from a conference at the nearby Convention Center. She and her friends went on a straight tequila run, excepting for Billy, who was sucking up Roy

Rogers like a dying desert rat. They'd lick the backs of their hands, sprinkle salt on the wet spot, lick it off, toss down the Cuervo Gold and bite into a lemon wedge, making a variety of not-pretty faces.

The Preacher, who'd fallen off the wagon for the blessed occasion, was telling Bubba about his adventures on an offshore oil rig that had exploded, sending him flying thirty-feet into the air to fortuitously land on a rubber life raft deployed by the oil company's safety officer.

"There I was. A sinner, Bubba. A certified, card-carrying student of the devil's workshop. A womanizing, cursing, impure-thinkin', drunken son-of-a-bitch with a death wish that was about to come true. Flyin' through the air like a clay pigeon, I had surrendered my soul to Satan."

He knocked back another shot of tequila without the ritual salt and lemon.

Bubba listened, nursing a Lone Star beer. The Preacher exhaled. " … Anyway, as I was sayin', me, a flea on the shag carpet of the Lord, I landed smack jim-iny in the life raft, on my back on top of Safety Officer Clinton." He paused. "Nice guy. I wonder what he done to deserve dyin' like that."

Stella and Billy were at the jukebox flipping through selections, Billy rattling the quarters that everybody had given him to be the party's jukebox D.J.

Gypsy and Patsy Mae were forehead to forehead in conversation. Gypsy lost track of how many tequilas Patsy had downed, figuring her friend was a little rummy after the marathon trip from the other side of the world. "Show me that ring again," Gypsy said. The flame from the votive candle on the bar hit the facets of the stones and made the ring dance with light.

"Nearly three carats," Patsy said. "Wish it wasn't my entire savings account." She looked down and then slowly raised her eyes to gypsy.

"You mean?"

"Yep – that's it. Kaput. What's in that suitcase in the back of ya'lls truck and this here ring, well, that's all I got. If you wouldn't have sent me that plane ticket, well, I'm not sure where I'd be." She crumbled up a cocktail napkin and pressed it to her eyes. "Figure I'll just sell this ol' ring and start over …. Sorry, didn't mean to dump this on you on your weddin' day."

Gypsy, who'd had a few shots, but not too many, put her arm around Patsy's shoulder. A carnation fell from her hair and landed in the salsa dish. "Honey, I am so sorry. What happened?"

"The man was an animal. He caught me by danglin' this big ol' ring in front of me, and I fell for it – went halfway around the dang world to get it. Then I found out he took it off some South African dope dealer in a card game, and all he wanted outta me was a maid to cook, clean, and give in to his manly desires. He treated me like one of his dang heifers. No, excuse me! He treated them better cause they sold by the pound." She sobbed and blew her nose in the napkin.

Gypsy handed her a tissue she'd had stuffed down the bodice of her dress to kind of "flesh out" her bosom. "There, there honey. You musta felt so alone, being in a different country and all. Poor Patsy Mae."

"I did, I did. Thankfully, Mr. McVee came along, and I had a little civilized company."

"Mr. McVee?"

"Nice old guy. Treated me wonderful, till his wife got home from her sister's in England." Patsy gave the bartender a nod.

"You drivin'?" he asked.

"No," Patsy snapped. "And mind your own damn business." She turned back to Gypsy with an apologetic smile. "Anyway, this is not your problem, it's mine. Men, with the exception of your Bubba, are your basic pond scum."

Gypsy noted to herself that any hint of Patsy's foreign accent had vanished in favor of the odd mix of a Louisiana, Alabama, Texas drawl. She was a little disappointed. Having an interesting and exotic friend was kind of a plus. "Ya'll just hang in there, Patsy. It'll be all right. Bubba and I will help you. Tomorrow is another day, I always say. You never know what's gonna happen."

"You are right, Gypsy Latreaux Smith," Patsy said, shaking herself out the mood she'd fallen into and raising her glass of shimmering gold liquor. "Here's to tomorrow cause today ain't too shabby and yesterday is plumb gone." They clinked shot glasses and performed the ritual, the tequila doing a slow burn on the way down.

"You be mindful of this stuff, Patsy Mae. It's not regular booze. It's got some kind of drug in it – something from a cactus, I think. Makes a girl crazy."

"Ain't cactus a vegetable? Like V8?" Patsy giggled. "I don't give a hoot nor a holler. I am broke as a broke-dick dawg, but I got a good friend in you."

Gypsy retrieved the carnation from the salsa dish and flicked off little pieces of tomato before shoving it back into her hairdo.

"So, you ever see one of them kangaroos?" she asked, thinking that changing the subject might lift Patsy's spirits.

"Kangaroos, wallaroos, buckaroos, I seen 'em all," Patsy said, giving the bartender the high sign. She turned back to Gypsy. "You know, I hate to ask you this, Gypsy, but while you and Bubba are on your honeymoon – do you think I could maybe house-sit? I don't exactly have a place to stay and, well, until I sell this here rock, I 'm a teensy bit short of funds."

"Well, you are in luck," Gypsy beamed. "We can sure do that. Me and Bubba are going off for three glorious nights at the Alamo Inn. I'll just give you the key, and you can make yourself right at home. Course, it ain't exactly a solid, anchored to God's-green-earth house, but it's a dang nice doublewide, and after I get my hands on it, it'll be a little piece of heaven.

Patsy Mae's face reddened. "You are just the best friend a gal ever had. The best … f-f-friend …" and tears welled up in her bloodshot eyes.

"Ya'll stop that now," Gypsy said. "My weddin' is no time for tears. Let's sing. Ya'll come over here, Stella. You too, Billy. Here's a quarter. Play B-5."

Bubba leaned back on the bar and watched as his wife pulled Stella to her right and Patsy to her left. Billy shuffled off and dropped the quarter in the slot, being extra careful to get the letter and number right. He'd had enough mishaps for one day. A soft instrumental drifted from the glowing box, and Gypsy tilted her head to listen. "Y'all back me up, ya hear? I like this version cause it ain't got no words. It's like havin' a whole band behind me." Soon the tune became familiar to everyone, and Gypsy let her eyes fall gently shut.

"Take this ribbon from my hair, set it loose and let it fall. All I'm askin' is your time. Help me make it through the night." Gypsy's voice rose over the small crowd in the bar and fell like misty rain on the few men and women in business suits, sipping martinis and glasses of white wine. They stopped their conversations and listened.

"I don't care what's right or wrong. I don't try to understand. Let the devil take tomorrow, tonight I need a helping hand." Up to the high notes, her voice lifted like a kite on a breeze. Back down to the deep, throaty notes. "Come and lay down by my side..."

A man in a three-piece suit stopped smoking his cigar and held it perched on his finger three inches from his waiting lips.

Patsy and Stella, who had tried to provide some back-up 'ooooohhs' and 'doo-whaass' had fallen silent. It was no longer Gypsy singing a familiar melody; she *was* the song. Patsy started to cry. Stella bit her lower lip.

Gypsy begged for the last time, "Help me make it through the night," holding the last note in a mournful breathiness that faded to silence. Silence that set her skin to tingling. Then, suddenly, applause erupted and, as if snapping out of a trance, she smiled and bowed her head like a true professional.

"Dang you," Stella said. "You about made me run my eyeliner, girl! That was downright beautiful." Patsy was still trying to compose herself, blowing her nose in a cocktail napkin, when the three-piece suit walked up. "Very fine singing, Ma'am," he said. "Allow me to introduce myself." He handed Gypsy a business card.

"I'm Carl Ventura, here for a conference of music per-
formers looking for an agent – which I am. And I am
very impressed."

"Well, thank you kindly, sir," Gypsy replied, glancing at the embossed business card. "I am Gypsy
Latreaux *Smith* and this here is my weddin' party, and
that gentleman is my brand new husband, Bubba."
Bubba slid off the barstool and joined the gaggle of
folks surrounding his bride.

Carl shook his hand, wincing from Bubba's grip.
"You have a very talented wife, congratulations."

"She can sing, all right, cain't she," Bubba said,
causing Gypsy to look at him in awe. She had not been
sure he'd noticed.

"So well that I'd like to have her pay me a visit at
my office. Maybe in a couple of weeks. Call me at that
number. Make an appointment."

Carl was dripping with confidence, good looks,
and very expensive clothes. Patsy Mae had quickly noticed these attributes and was repairing the damage
done to her face by all the sobbing. She dabbed her
nose with a cocktail napkin and reached out her hand,
palm down.

"And I am Patsy Mae, this talented lady's best friend. I came all the way from Australia just to be with her today." The Southern twang disappeared from her speech.

Carl took her outstretched hand and held it for a moment. "Pleased to meet you." Carl let himself smile, almost as if he'd remembered a joke. "Why don't you all come on over to our table. Let me buy the wedding party a drink."

Amid "Thanks," and "you don't have to do that" and other mumbling, Patsy and the Hill Country folk joined a small cadre of dressed-to-impress conventioneers. The fact that the two groups had little in common, other than an appreciation of the bride's vocal abilities, did not prove uncomfortable since everyone, except for Billy, was pretty well oiled-up. Patsy maneuvered herself to sit next to Carl, immediately sliding her hand under the table and switching the triple-crown ring from her left hand to her right.

Carl was the center of the universe – the three men and two women with him were young talent looking for an agent. Gypsy, being freshly married and thrilled that such a fine man had liked her singing, did not notice the occasional glares behind their uptown smiles.

And, when she revved up another tune, she asked them all to sing. It was as glorious a chorus as had ever graced the lounge at Friday's. As the singers belted out tunes – occasionally glancing to see if Carl was watching – Patsy was entertaining Carl with tales of life Down Under.

Gypsy had switched to Club Soda, and Bubba was slowly sipping a draught beer. He had pretty much been quiet since they'd moved to Carl's table. After Gypsy led a particularly fine rendition of "Mama He's Crazy," Bubba reached beneath the table and, in an unusual display of public affection, took her hand. "Just so ya know," he whispered in her ear, "I'll be getting' you that weddin' ring week after next – when ol' man Miller pays me for that deck job. Just so's ya know."

Gypsy was momentarily taken aback. She had already accepted the fact that it would be she who infused their relationship with romance, Bubba being the silent type. It was fundamental to her philosophy of "everything is a trade-off." Maybe this old dog could learn a few new tricks, she thought, giving her husband a bright smile. "That'd be mighty nice, sweetheart," she said, noticing Bubba's quick glance in Carl's direction and figuring a little competition could be a healthy thing. Bubba smiled back at her, looking like he'd just won a poker hand.

Carl, on the other hand, looked like a man needing air. Patsy Mae had moved in so close her elbow was resting on Carl's shrimp appetizer plate, and her breasts were caressing his left arm. The young blond woman on his other side was making her fingers walk up his right arm as she sang a familiar soap jingle into his ear. The others from the music conference were also competing for Carl's attention, and, for a moment, Gypsy felt sorry for the man.

The Preacher had taken to telling tales to Billy, who was trying to listen while helping Stella build a house out of the cardboard coasters. "That's when I saw her. In all her glory," the Preacher said to Billy.

"Saw who?" Billy asked, taking his eyes off the steeple of cards.

"The Blessed Virgin, that's who!"

"Oh."

"It was a miracle, I am tellin' you. There she was. Her face appearing as clear as the nose on your face. Of course, I could not eat that pancake. No, sir. I asked the manager at Denny's for a box so's I could take it to my church," the Preacher said, taking a slow sip of his drink and shaking his head. "Course, by the time I got it there, the syrup had all soaked into the pancake, and you couldn't make out her face like before. But I saw it. And, it was a sign."

"Of what?" Billy asked, leaning forward with interest and knocking Stella's four-tier tower down.

"Damned if I know. Still working on that, I am. You can't tune a revelation in like one of them satellite channels," said the Preacher.

"You can't?" Billy asked.

Stella, whose capacity for drink was a legend in the Hill Country, stood up and waved at the bartender. "One more," she shouted, raising her shot glass and looking at Gypsy. "Then, I gotta go. I have an urgent matter to attend to." That was the matter of the sequined dress that, as the evening wore on, was increasingly constricting circulation to her extremities. Drinks were ordered all around - beer, tequila, a Roy Rogers, a Club Soda for Gypsy and martinis, cosmopolitans, and scotch for Carl's crew. Patsy, intending to seal her bond with Carl, also ordered scotch, straight up.

Everybody stood and raised their glasses. The Preacher, being accustomed to presiding over momentous occasions, stared at his tall glass of honey-colored beer. "Here is a toast to Mr. and Mrs. Bubba and Gypsy Smith. May the good Lord bless and keep you and may your troubles be as few and as far apart as my grandma's teeth (may she rest in peace)."

Glasses met over the table and clinked in dissonant tones. Best wishes for Gypsy and Bubba issued forth, and drinks were downed. Billy forgot to remove the straw from his Coca Cola drink and poked himself in the eye, spilling most of the drink as his hand darted up to his face. Stella grabbed cocktail napkins to soak up the puddle on the table. "I'm sorry," Billy was sputtering. Stella reached up and wiped his hand off with a napkin.

"You're rubbin' soda into your eye, Billy," she said. Bubba gave him a comforting pat on the shoulder as the wedding party got ready to leave. Patsy Mae was urgently whispering something into Carl's ear when the Preacher's voice rose.

"Holy Jesus!" he exclaimed. "Holy Mother of God!" All eyes turned his way as he pointed to the glossy spill mark on the table. "There he is!"

"Who is?" Billy asked, peeking at the Preacher through one eye.

Stella picked up her purse. "He's seeing another one of them faces," she said with a tone of exasperation. "Who is it this time? Elvis?"

"Don't blaspheme, Stella!" the Preacher shot back at her. "Ya'll just look at that, and you tell me!"

The group huddled around the Preacher, except for Carl, who made a pistol with his thumb and index finger and pointed at Gypsy. "Call me," he mouthed and winked before slipping out the front door. Patsy Mae grabbed her purse and shot a quick look at Carl's back. She grinned.

"Well?" the Preacher asked again.

"Sure don't look like Elvis," Bubba offered with an amused tone. Mostly, the group was saying things like, "I don't see anything" and "where?"

Just as the Preacher started to outline what he saw as a tiny head and outstretched arms, Patsy Mae pulled Gypsy close and whispered into her ear. "Forget about that key to your place. I got a hot date. I'm slidin' outta here. Ya'll hang onto that bag of mine? I've got a mean old stretch Lincoln waiting for me curb-side!" Patsy had a little trouble with the consonants, having downed the better half of a bottle of Cuervo Gold before the shot of scotch.

"You think you should do this? After all, you just met the man," Gypsy said.

"Girl's gotta look out for nummer one," Patsy responded with a lazy wink. "Ya'll have a wonderful honeyroom. I mean moneyhoom. Whatever."

Gypsy's attention snapped back to the Preacher, who was announcing the identity of the spill vision. "It's the Baby Jesus. That's who it is. Here to bless the union of Bubba and Gypsy." By the time Gypsy turned back, Patsy Mae had taken off.

With Carl gone, the young singers from the conference felt no particular urge to be sociable and were howling with laughter about the Preacher. Bubba, who never did like folks making fun of others, gathered his buddies together and headed for the door. He walked with a certain pride, being aware that there were days in the past when he would have made a bunch of greenhorn wise-asses like that eat a fistful of teeth. That was before his court-ordered anger management classes. He'd come a ways, he mused.

Two-by-two they passed through the revolving glass door into the early evening. Billy, who had recovered from the straw incident, went through alone, making two complete revolutions before being pulled out to the street by Bubba.

The sun was just beginning to set, and the sidewalks of downtown Austin wore a soft pink glow. Gypsy linked her arm with Bubba's and they stood for a minute looking up at the tall buildings and down the grand street that led to the state's Capitol building basking in warm hues. There, about a quarter block up the avenue was a sleek black Lincoln. Shuffling unsteadily toward the Towne Car was Patsy Mae.

"I'll be," Bubba uttered. "I thought that music guy would bolt."

Patsy slapped the trunk of the Lincoln with the flat of her hand, and the driver stepped out. Stella let go of a laugh. "He did!" she said. "That's old Floutz's rig, and that's his driver."

They watched as the driver opened the back door of the car and Patsy Mae bent at the waist to crawl inside. She stopped halfway and looked inside, stood up, and glanced back at Gypsy. Patsy smiled and opened her arms in a gesture like the Preacher had seen in the liquid image of the Baby Jesus. "Whatever," she shouted and ducked into the back seat.

"Well, what do you know," Bubba said.

"I know one thing," Gypsy answered as she watched the elegant ride pull away from the curb.

"Any man who stands-up my best friend is no friend of mine." She reached into the bodice of her dress, re-trieved Carl's slightly damp card and ripped it in half.

2.
Crossing the Channel

It is a sun-filled day, and heat rises from the sand on the beach. Of course, being Frinton on Sea and facing the English Channel, there is still a nip of crispness in the air. There are few people here with me, and the cove seems intensely personal. This sense of solace does not change when a middle-aged couple slowly climbs down the rock stairs from the sea wall above and stand on the sand. They pause there, looking out, and I wonder if they will merely rest a while and leave. They look like tourists to the coast, a little surprised to find themselves here.

They are not dressed for the beach. She wears a pale blue sweater set and navy slacks. Her shoes have low heels. She holds a worn brown purse over her shoulder. He seems dressed for work, in a white shirt, and grey pants. Two pens protrude from the pocket of his shirt, and he unbuttons the sleeves and rolls them up a bit. They are not far from where I sit, book and camera in hand.

He says something softly to her, and she shakes her head. "No, I'll just stay here. You go ahead. I'd ruin my shoes," she tells him.

"Take them off," he suggests, smiling, playful.

She gives him a look of exasperation and waves him off like a mischievous puppy. Her hair is a chestnut color, likely covering a crop of unwanted grey. It has been recently styled, and she tries to pat it back into place as the breeze plays with it. After riffling in her purse, she pulls a thin white scarf out and ties it loosely around her head.

Her husband takes off his shoes, drops them in the sand, and strolls to the water's edge. He glances back at her, watching the ritual of saving her hairdo. His eyes are deeply blue like a fisherman's, and his face is etched with lines. I know this man is not a fisherman. His countenance hints of a desk job from which he is perhaps retired. Nonetheless, I picture him at ease here, alongside the sea, drawn to it almost without choice. I know he will wade in the water.

He walks beyond the damp line where the waves lap the shore. The man with hair the color of sea foam rolls up the legs of his pants and wanders in. His ankles are white as limestone. They are soon covered by water that laps up to his knees.

He stands and stares out over the Channel, his hands thrust into the pockets of his pants. He looks far southeast, and I wonder if he is reaching for memories of a week he'd spent at the beach long ago when he was young and full. He turns slightly as if to leave, but pauses instead and then inches out further into the tumbling surf.

After many minutes lost in his thoughts, he slowly walks back to his wife, who still stands on the stairs by the sea wall clutching her purse to her chest. "Come in with me?" he urges with a faint smile on his lips.

"I don't have a towel in the car," she answers, clearly unwilling to join her husband in his rite with the water. "Go ahead. Don't worry about me."

He takes off his watch and hands it to his wife. He turns his back to her again and walks directly into the water, the forward thrust splashing his trousers, making dark wet spots. The surf is gentle and laps up against legs so thin they look as if they might snap if hit by a strong wave.

Behind him, on the beach, two lovers lay entwined on a red blanket pressed into the sand like a nest. The young woman with hair the color of honey, quickly sits up and laughs at some words she and her lover have shared. The sound peals like a bell, riding over the sand and out to sea. Her long hair dances in the wind, and she runs her fingers through it. The man reaches up and grabs her arm, pulling her down against him again until they are wrapped around each other, touching from toe to head. They are dressed for touching, she wearing a deep back-less swimsuit, and he in brief trunks that shimmer when he moves.

The older man wrests his gaze from the horizon and turns to look at his wife.

"It's warm," he shouts over the low roar of the surf and the laughter of the young couple. "It's not at all cold!"

His wife shifts her purse to her hip, raises her chin, and answers, "That's nice," still not drawn to join him in his baptism of salt and foam. She will stand patiently, without complaint, and wait until her husband tires of

the moment. He is quite wet by now, and she waves at
him in a gesture of tolerance for his frivolity. She shakes
her head slightly, like a mother watching a precocious
child.

As the man looks at his wife, and she at him, his gaze
falls upon the young couple in the sand. He is of a gener-
ation that is loathe to stare, but he watches them nonetheless. I see his chest rise and fall in an exaggerated sigh.
The look on his face is not disapproving, but softly sor-
rowful. His wife has pinched her mouth up like a closed
blossom. She gives no sign she's seen the young couple at
all though I know she has glanced, perhaps more than
once. She gazes briefly at me and then up at the sea wall
and back out to out to the water.

The young lovers are oblivious to the older couple.
Oblivious, in fact, to everything save their mutual bodies
and fervor for each other. They roll over so she is now on
top, her hair caressing her lover's face like strands of
windblown silk. His arms, flecked with tiny grains of
sand, shimmer in the sunlight as he moves his hands over
her bare back. I wonder what stops them from coupling
there on the beach in front of us, each with our own re-
flections of youth and passion.

The husband reaches down and scoops up a handful

of water. He wipes his face and lets the drops fall to his white shirt. I see him taste the salt on his lips before turning and facing the endless sea. His wife's eyes have drifted fully to the lovers and she watches them with curiosity, her head tilted to one side and lips slightly parted as if preparing to ask a question.

The day has been uncharacteristically bright and warm, but clouds have gathered and now obscure the late afternoon sun. Without the sun's reflection on the sand, the beach loses its warmth. It is a signal for the husband to turn his back on the eastern horizon and allow his legs to dry in the breeze.

He pushes his way through the waves, past the young couple, digging his toes into the sand as he walks to his wife's side. They stand together for a moment looking out at the sea, over the lovers who seem unaware of the change in climate. Where they touch each other there is no room for chill, they are an envelope of warmth They defy the passage of time, of temperature, perhaps, even, the turning of the earth.

The husband puts his arm around his wife's shoulder. "Cold?" he asks.

"Getting there," she answers. "Back to the car then?" She hands him his watch and helps him fasten it around his wrist. He watches her face as she tucks away the loose end of the band. They turn and climb the worn stairs of the seawall to the cliffs above. I follow at a distance and listen. Wanting something for them, from them.

They don't talk as they walk the path along the sea-wall edge. There are wildflowers here and there, and benches built of weathered wood overlooking the expansive view of the Channel. They pause at one bearing an inscription etched in brass. It is the woman's voice. "In loving memory of my husband and friend, Len Cherry, whose eyes were as blue as the sea and heart as deep."

"Yes, well," said the man looking out at the half-circle of sun peeking from the clouds and touching the back of the bench with warm light. "He must have been quite a fellow."

His wife, feeling the bite of the wind and looking in his eyes, answers by hooking her arm in his and pulling her husband closer. She looks up into his eyes and smiles. "Come on. Let's get you to the car. You're soaked. "

I rest on Len Cherry's bench and watch the young lovers sit up and gaze out to sea. The clouds have parted. The waning sun hits them, and their bodies cast long shadows in the sand.

3.
The Attic

The white, wood-frame house stood on the knoll of a hill at the end of steep, winding dirt road that washed out with every spring thaw. For Trish and Mark, it was an adventure not often experienced by their family, that ride up the slippery mud with Gramma clutching the padded armrest of the Buick until her knuckles turned white.

"Take it easy Frank. Frank! Be careful or we'll go right off the road," she'd cry, and Papa Frank would just remain silent and pilot the 1958 two-toned grey coupe around the slick hairpin turns and through the ruts and gullies until the car humped over the last crest and onto the farm. The kids and their mother sat in the back seat, the grandparents in the front. Trish favored the window on the driver's side, wanting to be fully informed should the car one day slide off the road and down the grassy hill into unseen, unimagined horrors of the shadowy landscape of rocks and trees.

The ride to Aunt Mary and Uncle Felix's farm deep in the hills of Minnesota skirting the wide Mississippi River was a departure from life in the family home in Winona. Since her father had been gone, Trish and her little brother, a curly-haired three-year-old, had lived with her grandparents and her mother in the river town where every other kid had a dad, and divorce was as uncommon as sunshine in February. It was necessarily a conservative family life, where no one took chances or called unnecessary attention to themselves. A half dozen times or so a year, they left the river town behind and spent the day where the calendar seemed to have stopped somewhere around 1925.

Aunt Mary was her grandmother's older sister - a religious woman who practiced her own brand of Catholicism, and who Trish never saw without an apron wrapped around her broad waist. She and Uncle Felix lived like people from a history book— no electricity, running water, or plumbing. Aunt Mary cooked on an old cast iron woodstove, food was kept in an underground pantry, a chamber pot was tucked under the bed, and a wooden barrel for churning butter sat in the corner of the kitchen.

The wild ride up the rutted road was the only portal to this place from the past with an atmosphere that made life in a small town like Winona, seem boring in comparison. Trish felt anticipation and fear the minute she jumped from the car and looked at the old farm with its out-buildings surrounded by forestland that grew poison ivy and other evil weeds that could make children sick or, according to her gramma, dead.

She and Mark were not allowed to penetrate the border of the overgrown hillsides. Safe territory was limited to where the adults could keep an eye on them. Which is precisely why Trish loved to explore the leaning clapboard buildings that housed machinery, tools, animals and, she supposed, secrets.

In the chicken coop, she definitely felt an inexplicable danger. There, among the boxes of warm eggs and feathers that drifted on the slightest breeze, with sunlight streaming through the cracks in the walls and the smell of chickens choking-out the fresh country air, she was wary. Nervous. Constantly looking over her shoulder. If a hen for no good reason - because chickens, her uncle had said, were very, very stupid - should be suddenly startled and spring into the air squawking and screeching, Trish would jump and run from the coop straight into the bright kitchen of the farmhouse. No matter that Uncle Felix told them never to run around Shep, the great collie who protected the farm and its living things. The danger that hung in the atmosphere inside the chicken coop was more terrifying than Shep's pointy teeth.

Trish preferred to play outside because the adults were hugely uninteresting with their talk of relatives and how poorly some of them were doing down in the city. And, if they were talking about something that just might be interesting, her grandmother and great Aunt lapsed quickly into Polish, leaving the rest of the family to only imagine what scandal they might be airing.

A simple white, clapboard house dominated the hilltop, seeming much larger than it was, with a grand front porch, a root cellar with double doors that were latched shut to keep children out and, Trish imagined, the cellar monsters in. A respectable distance from the house was the outhouse, an ancient barn that leaned to one side, and threated to collapse at the slightest urging from man or nature, and the teeming chicken coop surrounded by a platoon of flying insects. There was also a small deteriorating garage that housed a rusting Model T pickup truck that her uncle, on rare occasion, drove down the hill to the nearest town.

The outhouse smelled horrible and was filled with noisy flies the size of bumblebees. Trish once held her breath, peeked down the hole, and saw no bottom at all. Perhaps, she thought, it led to Hell or a den of snakes. The outhouse wasn't an option for adventure, and Uncle Felix had forbidden her to go inside the cavernous rust-red barn that housed two milk cows. The cows, he said, could kill a child with one kick. They were about as dumb as chickens, he said. Besides, the barn wasn't safe. The timbers were old and leaning. The loft hung down like an open jaw, spilling bales of hay onto the dirt floor.

Not too far from the house was a water well with a long handled pump. The water was always cold and tasted crisp and alive. But for some unknown reason, the well was declared dangerous, and an adult had to be outside when Trish went to draw a ladle of water. More than once, she tried to discover what was so perilous about the pump and well, but had quickly been herded indoors by an adult.

The best outdoor place was the front porch or, more specifically, under the front porch where passels of kittens were produced like a seasonal crop. Born of wild mothers who hid them deep beneath the house, it was a perennial challenge to catch a kitten and quiet its instinctual fears. Most often, they bared their needle-sharp baby fangs and struck out with virgin claws that left bleeding red welts on Trish's arms. The consistent result of kitten-catching, nonetheless, did not deter Trish from the hunt.

Trish managed to stay away from the sloping hillside where other animals waited to catch an unwary child. There were snakes. Water Moccasins and Rattlers. She could picture them striking out at her bare legs, locking down and never letting go. There were also giant poisoned mushrooms on the hill. She believed that just touching them was enough to send a child into fits that ended in a feverish death. Aunt Mary assured her this was true.

Indeed, most outdoor adventures ended with her bolting into the house where the air was hot and dry and smelled of baking bread. There, she felt safer, not because of the house itself, but because the adults were nearby. In fact, the house presented its own problems that were, in some ways, more frightening than crazed chickens or cows that wanted to kill children. Trish could never identify exactly what was wrong because she realized it was something that couldn't be seen.

There was the dining room where the adults sat and gossiped, her mother bouncing little Mark on her knee. There was nothing frightening about the massive wooden table or sideboard where delicate china cups were displayed around a set of silver salt and pepper shakers shaped like pheasants. And framed prints of the baby Jesus and the Virgin Mary, the Last Supper and Pope Pius XII that hung on the walls along with palm fronds twisted into a dry braid should have been comforting but were, instead, unsettling. There was also the bowl of Holy Water that sat on a little stand near the entry to her aunt's bedroom, which was drenched in inviting afternoon sunlight.

The bedroom was small and crowded with massive furniture. A feather-filled quilt was piled high on a brass bed so tall, Trish could barely see over the top. There was a towering wooden chest where Aunt Mary hung her clothes, and Trish sometimes hid when she wanted to play tricks on the adults. On another ornate wooden dresser was a kerosene lamp, and dozens of Holy Cards propped up against a statue of the Virgin Mary. A large, carved crucifix hung on the wall opposite the bed with more palm fronds tucked artfully behind. At the foot of the bed was a cedar chest holding an old picture album with a ruby red velvet cover. Inside were black and white photos of men with beards and women wearing bustles and high necked, dark dresses. There was also a picture of a baby lying in a coffin. Trish held her breath each time she turned a page in fear of coming across the photo, which she did on every visit to the farm.

Around the corner from the bedroom was a narrow and dark hallway. Aunt Mary had a treadle sewing machine tucked in the corner and baskets of sewing on the floor. At the far doorway sat a small table with another dish of Holy Water and a rosary lovingly waiting for someone's prayers. Trish always stopped at this dish, touched the water with her index and middle fingers and made the Sign of the Cross on her body before moving to pass and pause in front of the stairs to the attic - a place that both frightened and attracted her. The Holy Water, she felt, gave her protection from something unknown and potentially dangerous that lived up there. She sometimes dashed purposely past the stairs and straight into the kitchen with its black, cast- iron cookstove and bright yellow walls. The kitchen felt entirely safe even though the entrance to the root cellar was right under a small braided rug in the middle of the floor. It was another place she was forbidden to go.

The attic was another place that was off-limits to children. She had been sternly warned away from the stairs. There had been no explanation, just a finger-wagging at the end of mother's arm while the other adults looked on and nodded their heads in agreement. "Don't climb up those stairs. There is nothing up there for you. Do you understand me? If I catch you disobeying, you know what will happen."

Yes, and no. Trish knew it would be something really unpleasant, but she'd never pushed far enough to find out what "what" actually was. And she wasn't thinking about the possible repercussions when she paused at the foot of the stairs one August visit and let her eyes climb them, one by one, up to a gaping rectangle where silvery specks of dust danced about in thin beams of sunlight coming from somewhere in the attic. Trish stood still as the statue of the Virgin Mary on her Aunt's dresser, and, slowly, she began to feel something.

At first, she sensed an urge to run and knew that, if she took flight, she would no longer be able to make her customary round of the house. Never be able to safely pass this spot again. Her wary decision to stand fast let a new sensation surround her, enter her body like the slender arm of a spirit flowing from the rafters of the attic, down the stairs, and into her being. It was as if gravity had changed its course and was pulling upwards into the place that children should never go. Where adults had hidden away a secret so dark that, if young eyes were to look upon it, something unthinkable, indeed unimaginable, would forever change the course of the child's life.

Trish knew this, and still, she placed her foot with its red, canvas tennis shoe on the first step. She let her right hand touch the cool wall and made a tight fist with her left. Eyes locked on the envelope of light at the top of the stairs she climbed, pausing on each step to listen and to feel. Midway, one of the steps groaned beneath her weight and she froze, thinking that someone in the dining room had heard and would come storming around the corner. She held her breath and squeezed her eyes shut until it was clear the adults had not noticed the nearly human sound that echoed in the stairwell.

With greater care, she lifted herself to the next step, which let loose with a high pitched scream, not unlike the sound of a captured wild kitten. Again, she held her breath and waited. She gingerly tested the next step and found that it too, was waiting to release an unearthly sound. Caught in the middle of an ancient keyboard, Trish thought about backing down the stairs. But, she risked making the same noises again on the way down, and the attic opening was only four more steps away.

Filling her lungs with air, she breathed out like an athlete, sending floating specks of dust into a whirlwind that spiraled up into the ether. Trish watched the particles ascend and made her decision. She catapulted up the remaining stairs like a frightened animal bolting to safety, though she had no idea whether shelter or peril awaited her there.

Trish landed on her hands and knees and quickly turned herself around to survey the mysterious room that was off-limits to all children. Afternoon sunlight poured in from square windows at each end of the peaked roof and through the many cracks in the walls where the weathered boards had split and twisted. Cobwebs hung like lace from dark wooden rafters. There were sharp angles where the roof met the floor that no light penetrated, where shadowy, indiscernible objects stared back at Trish.

She looked to the peak of the ceiling rafters and examined the odd shapes that seemed to be glued to the beam. Slowly it dawned on her that bats had claimed the attic for daylight sleeping, and she unconsciously ducked (She lived with the nightmare of having a mad bat stuck in her hair, wildly flapping and biting. Rabid bats that, her grandmother had told her, would cause a person to have painful shots right in the stomach before they died foaming at the mouth). But Trish figured that bats only flew at night and, chances were, she'd be alright so long as the sun shone in the windows.

At the far end of the attic was a pile covered with a white sheet. This, she thought, was what children were not supposed to see, and it drew her like a powerful magnet. She quickly calculated the risks of making the trek across the floorboards, which were missing in some places and broken in others. One wrong step and she could fall through the ceiling, maybe directly onto the dining room table and into the adult conversation. Even without that happening, the old floor was bound moan beneath her weight.

Trish moved onto her hands and knees and slowly, carefully began to crawl. She tried to distribute her weight evenly among her arms and legs to lessen the impact. Moving like a mud turtle, Trish heard only the tiniest of creaks from the boards beneath her, and she began to sweat with the effort of concentration. It was near the end of the afternoon, and the heat from the day had risen to the attic making it hard to breathe. She felt trapped in a triangle of stillness shared with bats and spiders and, yes, something else. She looked back to find the opening to the stairs, half afraid it may have disappeared and, reassured, crept forward the final few feet.

The covered pile was about the size of a dog house, with irregular shapes making the contour of the sheet take on a form that obscured the nature of things beneath it. She touched a rounded portion. It was soft like a pillow. Feeling the rest with her open hands, she forgot about escaping or falling into the laps of adults. The collection under the sheet absorbed her attention as she tried to guess what secret might be hidden beneath it.

Trish leaned her head down to the floor and lifted up the frayed corner of the sheet which, she noticed, had been embroidered like other linens in Aunt's Mary's house. She saw wooden rockers and something else that appeared to be made of fur. Unable to resist any longer, she raised the sheet and raised up on her knees. There beneath her arms in the shadow of the tent she'd made was a stuffed toy bear with dark eyes that gleamed, even in the dim light. She reached out and picked it up. Soft, softer than any stuffed toy she'd ever touched. Trish petted it as if it was a kitten and looked more closely at the rocking cradle.

It took a moment or two for what she saw to register. There, in the cradle, was a baby-sized bundle completely swathed in a tight, yellowed wrap. Trish felt it, and through the fabric the object inside yielded to her touch. A baby, a real baby, she knew and was paralyzed with the realization. She let the sheet drop from her hand and hovered helplessly over the horrible secret.

Suddenly, information came together in a great and awful realization. Aunt Mary had stolen a baby and wrapped it in a shroud in the attic. The softness of the bear in her arms became clear to her in the very same moment. To keep the stolen baby company, her aunt had skinned the wild kittens and made a stuffed toy.

Trish tried to gather her wits. If she should be caught with such dark knowledge, her life would be in peril. It was important to leave everything as she'd found it. Repulsed and horrified, she put the bear back beside the baby and smoothed out the sheet. Unwilling to turn her back on the mound, she began a slow and sometimes painful backward crawl toward the stairs, toward the kitchen and porch and barnyard that would never again feel the same.

At the edge of the opening, she stopped and listened. There were voices coming from below. "Trish, Trish?" her mother was calling. "Trish, where are you, we're getting ready to go!"

Aunt Mary joined her mother in the kitchen. "I thought I saw her walking around here like she always does," Auntie said. "She didn't crawl under my bed, did she? You know how that girl likes to cause a fuss." Footsteps moved into the bedroom, where no child was discovered under the bed.

"Maybe she went back outside," her mother said. "She's forever chasing those kittens."

"I'll check the chicken coop," Uncle Felix was saying. "I think she's a lil' afraid of those critters, but seems to me she can't stay away from `em."

Trish heard the screen door slam shut and started to inch her way down the stairs. Suddenly there were sounds in the kitchen. Aunt Mary must have stayed inside to start the woodstove fire for dinner. Trish backed up the stairs, out of sight. She looked over toward the pile looming in the attic. The sun had started to sink behind the hill, and it was quickly getting darker. Soon, she knew, the bats would awaken. She would entombed in the pitch-black night with creatures, living and dead, too awful to contemplate.

Mother and Uncle Felix came back inside. Concern entered their voices. "I don't see her out there," Uncle said.

"She's not under the porch, I got on my hands and knees and looked," Mother was saying. "Do you think she could have gone to the barn?"

By then, the rest of the family was also in the kitchen, venturing guesses about where Trish could have gone. "I checked the well," Uncle Felix said somberly. "I always worry about that. Nobody's been messin' with it."

"Maybe she went to see the cows," Grandma offered. "She just loves animals."

"Just so she didn't wander out on the hillside," Grampa Frank said.

"Maybe she's shut herself in the outhouse," Aunt Mary suggested.

"Oh, dear," Mother sighed. Trish could imagine how her mom was probably standing bolt upright and covering her mouth with her hand like she always did when she was worried.

If it hadn't been for the extreme awfulness of the discovery, if Trish had only found boxes of bad magazines or whiskey bottles in the attic, she would have given herself up. Instead, she kneeled where she was, put her hands together and said a Hail Mary, silently moving her lips with the words.

"Let's all go look for her," Grampa was saying. "Felix, you go to the barn and be sure to check up in the loft. That girl loves to climb. I'll head down the road, and the women can walk around the yard, check that outhouse."

Trish heard Aunt Mary replacing the cast iron burner on the stove, and soon the screen doors in the kitchen and the dining room slammed shut. She bolted from her perch and slid down the stairs. Trish knew it would cause trouble, but she picked another forbidden spot for hiding. She quickly raised the door to the root cellar and sat on the crooked cement steps. In the momentary light from above, she saw that her uncle had killed a couple of chickens and hung them from the rafters. The bloody hatchet leaned against the dirt wall. Trish inched the rug over the opening as best she could from below and let the hatch slam shut. She crouched on the cold step and started to recite the *Act of Contrition* that could save a person's soul should they die unexpectedly. The chickens dangled silently behind her.

It seemed like hours before the search party returned. "Where can she be?" her mother intoned. "I'm just so worried!"

Trish made her entrance as boldly as possible for a girl who had just faced death. She popped open the hatch on the floor and said, "Here I am! I bet you couldn't find me!" She plastered a weak smile on her face as Grampa hauled her out of the hole by one arm.

"You had us worried sick," he barked. Since Grampa Frank was always a soft-spoken gentleman, Trish knew serious trouble was ahead.

"What do you think you're doing?!" Mother demanding, holding Marky on her hip and drawing Trish to her side. "I told you to never go into the cellar!"

"Don't be too hard on her," Aunt Mary said. "She looks a little scared to me. Did you get frightened down there, honey?" Trish sunk further into the folds of her mother's dress to avoid her aunt's caress.

"Surprised she'd stay down there, what with those hens and all," Uncle Felix said with a thin grin on his face.

"Well, this won't be forgotten. I told you what would happen if you disobeyed," Mother said a little less harshly.

The sun was beginning to set, and the family headed for the car. It was the custom for Aunt Mary to get a goodbye hug from the children. She leaned down and looked deeply into Trish's eyes, so deeply Trish felt the look on the souls of her feet.

"You know, honey, I had a dream about you, and your little brother," she said breathing warmly on Trish. "I dreamed you both were with Jesus. You were on his right side, and Marky was on his left. You're such little angels." She squeezed Trish's arm extra hard and hugged her tight to her soft bosom. Trish wondered if the baby in the attic had suffocated.

The Buick wound safely down the dirt driveway and onto the one-lane blacktop road. Trish looked out the back window to the top of the hill. As usual, Aunt Mary stood at the edge of the ridge and waved a white handkerchief over her head as the family car headed back down the winding road to the city. Murderer, Trish thought as she fought back tears.

The ride home was calm and quiet. No one had

much to say. Trish's punishment had begun with the news that she would not be able to play outside for an entire week. There would be more to come, her mother threatened. It didn't matter to Trish because, after today, life would never be the same anyway.

At school that September, Trish became more quiet than she had been in the past. Her teachers commented on how nice the change was. Trish just wasn't any trouble for them. She wasn't repeatedly talking or breaking rules. She'd stopped bothering her classmates and seemed to be a more serious student. "She appears to have matured over the summer," her teacher, Sister Audrey, said.

Soon, the first snow came, and it was again impossible to make the trip into the country and up the road to visit Aunt Mary. It would be late spring when the family would pile into the car and head for the hills. By then, Trish figured she would have run away from home. Maybe with the Ringling Brothers Circus whose trains ran on the rails across the street from her house. She could no longer visit Aunt Mary and, since refusing to make a family excursion was out of the question, leaving home was the only choice.

Trish made her plans as winter descended upon the

town and buried the street and railroad tracks in mounds of thick, white snow. By Christmas vacation the first blizzard had come, and families were trapped inside small houses with Ed Sullivan filling Sunday nights with visions of glamour and faraway cities of laughing, dancing people with sparkling eyes—a life totally different from her own. Snowbound and living with a dark secret, she imagined disappearing behind the black and white TV screen.

She sat down for supper at five o'clock each night and faced her family silently. Mark was the only one she played with or really talked to, and after all, he didn't understand a thing she was saying. He was like the baby doll she'd once wanted for Christmas. The soft, realistic doll she'd seen in the Sears Catalogue. Her very own baby to love. But that was before the attic. Before the responsibility she now carried like a sack of black coal.

Christmas Eve, she cried again, as she had done so many nights since August. And again, she put herself to sleep by inventing a beautiful story in her head. Trish had the ability to visually picture the whole tableau, and it made her calm, sleepy. In it she dreamed of meeting a young man at the circus and discovering he was with the High Flying Sandini Family. He took her atop the swinging rope ladder onto a narrow platform, and there she fearlessly grasped the metal bar of the trapeze and flew effortlessly into space. She arched her back and looked ahead. The young man (he had no name) was there, reaching out to catch her. Trusting him, she let go of the trapeze and flew to his outstretched hands. Back and forth they flew, Trish learning quickly and turning somersaults in the air. Him catching her and smiling. The crowd cheering. Trish daring to do more and more. And so she would fall asleep with visions of danger and drama and safety playing on the colored screen in her mind.

Christmas morning dawned like no other before or after. Ordinarily, Trish would have tried to remain awake the night before so that she could peek out her bedroom door in the hope of catching sight of the adults hauling presents down from the attic. She had initially been crushed when she first discovered that it was not Santa stealing in at midnight to scatter packages under the tree. Her first stealthy crawl from the bedroom down the hall to spy on Christmas Eve had been at the tender age of five. But now, three years later, she'd accepted the truth and was no longer disappointed. This year she lacked the motivation to get out of bed at all.

Trish heard her mother calling. "Trish, it's Christmas.

Come see what Santa left you! Trish, come on! What's the matter with you?"

Trish slipped on her pink robe and fuzzy slippers. She also put on the best face she could, given the circumstances. She entered the living room where her little brother was already ripping away at a package. "Wait Marky," her mother was saying. "We have to do this in order. Just wait your turn. Trish, just look what Santa left for some good little girl."

There, unwrapped, centered under the tree, was a magnificent carved cradle holding a baby doll and a silky brown teddy bear. The doll was exactly what Trish had asked for so many months before - soft to the touch like a real baby. "The bear is very, very special too," Trish's mom was saying. "It's made of genuine rabbit fur. Now you be careful with it. It's not to be taken outside."

Rabbit fur, Trish thought, as she hugged the doll and buried her face in the softness of the bear. Not kitten fur. She started to cry into the bear's big silky tummy. "Trish, don't do that. You'll ruin the fur!" her mother said. "Trish, what in the world is wrong with you? Aren't you happy?"

3.
A New Year on the Rails

New Year's day, damp with a sky of foggy pewter. It was the perfect environment to be in my second floor studio, playing with clay and imagination. I needed the solitary break. It had been a holiday filled with drama, mostly related to family, as the season seems to invite.

I was ready to begin anew and put a year of too many visits to hospitals and too many funerals behind me. A day in my artistic aerie, particularly a day with such gray pallor seemed the perfect transition.

A mound of clay sat in front of me. By mid afternoon I trusted it would be something entirely different and felt an anticipation of satisfaction and, well, triumph that comes with the act of creating. I looked at my rustic little space that's surrounded on three sides by windows. I see the tops of trees and roofs of houses, neighbors' back-yards and, most prominently, the railroad tracks that de-marcate the city from the wilds of the riverfront. Just over the tracks hawks nest in trees, skunks and coyotes scurry under the brush. Beavers carve fallen logs into flesh col-ored totem poles, and it's possible to forget the city, its freeways, its hospitals, our manmade cares and concerns.

In my studio I can invite nature in. It's present with me as I clean my tools and look at the clay, plotting my point of attack. Visualizing how the picture in my head will become three dimensional. My fingers dig deep into the unformed five-pound block and I feel free of adult conventions. I'm a kid with dirty fingernails, playing in the mud.

I grab a handful of the moist, gritty clay that's made of recycled papers and earth, and start to build a pur-poseful mound. Over the morning, I add clay and then take my tools and carve away to find what's hidden there for me.

I stop to watch a freight train as it barrels along the tracks. I like to imagine where the cargo containers have been and where they might be going. I remember being a child, growing up a half block from the railroad tracks, and feeling grateful for the trains because they were proof that there was a much larger world than the one that trapped me so thoroughly in my tiny Midwestern town with too many people in a tiny house.

The boxcars and flatcars sped through places like New York, Chicago. They might be on their way to California or maybe to Canada. They were getting out of town. Unlike me, they were free to leave.

The trains were also a source of extreme danger. Every year, someone was killed by a train, whether by accident or by design, it made little difference. I'd fanaticize about standing there in the middle of the tracks and watching the massive engine roar toward me carrying instant death as its load. Ricky Busack, a teenage friend, had done just that. It was the first funeral I'd ever attended. Since I knew him and had talked to him on the phone just days before he'd taken his own life, I felt responsible.

As a kid, I'd also flirted with the terrors of the tracks. I laid my ear down on the silver cold steel to see if I could hear the hum of an oncoming train, all the while fully expecting to look up and see it swallowing me under its towering engine to be shredded and crushed by the concave metal wheels.

I thought of these things as I looked up from the round little body that was emerging from my lump of clay and wished away the morose thoughts.

Small wonder that I should go that route. It had been only three days since my husband and I discovered our renter, limp, and nearly lifeless in a lounger inside the tiny blockhouse he called home. As we called 911 and got emergency instructions, we both knew it was the suicide attempt he'd threatened weeks before.

He'd stopped breathing, but I could feel a pulse. I listened to the dispatcher on the phone and did CPR, 100 beats, she told me. After 70, he gasped and took in some air, and then stopped breathing again. And so it went until the EMTs arrived. Dead, alive and back again. It was touch and go, but he made it. Just months later, he succeeded in his effort to exit life.

Banish that thought, too! I turned on the radio to soft music and steered my mind to other concerns. Should I give this piece a glaze treatment or use stains? Should the character be a female or genderless? Is it better without a lot of detail?

It was early afternoon when I again looked up and out at my landscape. Directly to my left, not a half-block away, a young man sat with a guitar on the tracks. His back was to the river and feet planted between the rails. He was playing the guitar, looking downward. I watched him, willing him to look up and see me. See that I could see him.

Probably nothing, I thought. A romantic New Year notion – to sit on the tracks and compose a ballad. He stopped playing and got on a cell phone. Good, he's chatting with a friend.

I went back to work on the piece, occasionally glancing up to watch him play his guitar or look west along the tracks. I was bothered. A train hadn't come since morning, and one was due late afternoon. I knew that engineers dreaded seeing people on the tracks – forcing them to try to control tons of speeding steel. What a crappy thing to do another person, a selfish act. I thought about shouting out the window at him, but talked myself down.

I sat there in conflict for 90 minutes more. Then, I called 911. Bad for the workers on the train. Bad for the young man. The dispatcher said they'd send a car. With butterflies in my stomach, I went back to my fanciful creature and kept track of time. It had been three hours since I'd noticed him, and still, he sat, only occasionally standing and pacing between the rails, looking west.

By 4 p.m., the already dim light began to fade. No police had come, and the slight young man in his black jacket and knit cap was still there. I began cleaning my tools, spraying the piece with water, and wrapping it in plastic to keep it from drying out too fast. I caught movement in the corner of my eye and saw him stand to hoist the guitar over his shoulder. He turned around and looked up. I willed him to see me, so he'd know he hadn't been alone. I want to believe we locked eyes for a moment. Then he turned and walked east, down the center of the tracks. I watched him till he paused about a block away. I wanted him to take the worn path down the embankment to the safety of the neighborhood. But he just stood there.

From downstairs, my husband shouted that it was time to leave. As I pulled down the shades on my windows, I saw the man had turned back and was walking west, towards the setting sun. No police, no train all afternoon.

We set the house alarm and locked the front door. In the distance, I heard the wail of the train whistle, a lonely echo that preceded a soft rumble beneath my feet. As we drove away from the house, a police car rounded the corner. The roar of the freight train, its diesel-stained engine pulling hundreds of tons of payload on spinning wheels of steel, appeared on the western horizon. I looked desperately for the silhouette of my afternoon companion, but could only see the triangle of bright headlights on the engine. I stood frozen, hoping I would not hear the scream of air brakes. Wanting him to have walked down the bank and into the warren of warehouses that lay beneath the tracks.

I thought about going to talk to the police who'd pulled to the end of the street beneath the tracks. The train barreled past, making the ground rumble under its weight, sending deafening sound waves into the night air. No desperate screech of iron and steel. And, on second thought, no need to alert the police. I figured the young man didn't need any trouble after his afternoon of contemplation. At least for today, the first day of his new year, he'd chosen life.

4.
The Conversation

NOT too bad this morning. The grass was dry. Probably has something to do with why I'm not aching in the small part of my back as much as last week with those colder nights and dew on the ground. Of course, it also helps that I got rid of that darn suitcase that do-gooder gave to me. Thing was really awkward to drag around – and heavy. Hard to roll over the grass and gravel. But then, they were made for rolling on shiny cement surfaces in airports, weren't they ... You remember that, don't you? The lovely airports with the restaurants and busy, important people. Was I important? I went first class, what, two or three times? Naw, that doesn't mean I was important. What's important anyway?

Whoa! There, that's important. Thank you, picnickers! A perfectly good plastic bag … trash bag. Heavy, not disgusting inside, no nasty food smell. And what's this? A whole treasure chest of cans, soda cans. Must have been a family. So much better than a bunch of beer drinkers who leave cigarette butts in the cans and whatnot. They don't even use the recycling bin half the time. Just chuck 'em in the garbage or on the ground. Anyway, good find!

Looks to be about nine. Yep, that's right. There she is, at the curtain like clockwork. …

Recycling center opens at 10. Should be able to hit there, then get over to Sutter Park by 10 if I keep a move on it. Don't want to get stuck in a line and have to talk to some of the crazies. Or get stuck next to one of the really stinky ones. No matter how long I'm out here I swear I'll never get used to that, and no matter how bad it gets, I'll never go there – not wash or try to get clean. Get used to smelling like an old skunk – something that's not even human.

Yeah, they can treat you like that – like a dog or even worse (some dogs in this town have it pretty sweet), but you don't have to buy it. I'm still a human. A human being and I plan to act like one.

IT LOOKS like another hot one. Doesn't seem to have cooled off much last night. But it's probably cool enough to open some windows till about 10 or 11. Before it heats up. Fresh air. Always a good way to start out the day.

There she is. I wonder where she slept last night. One of the shelters? I hear there is usually a place, a bed, for women. Not for single men, but for women and children. I wonder what she did with her stuff. She had it in a big suitcase – a black one with, what was it? Silver spots spray-painted on it so a previous owner could find it easier on the baggage carousel.

"Jasper! Stop that barking! It's nothing. Just that poor homeless lady in the park. Save those barkies for the really bad guys. Okay, sweetums? Mummy make you breakfast in a minute."

Maybe it was stolen. Somebody took the bag and all her stuff. Must be really tough. She must literally live out of that backpack now. I don't know how they do it.

What time is it? Oops, so much for a cooked breakfast. Dr. Phil. A croissant, some of that cranberry jam, coffee … do I have Smart Balance left? Well, a little butter never hurt anyone.

Gawd, she's picking though the trash. I'm surprised she doesn't get something. I wonder if exposure to germs and bacteria raises your immunity.

"Jasper, drop it! Yuk! Bad! You got that out of the garbage can, bad boy. Here, give it to me. Mummy open nice new can of beef and gravy for her precious."

LUNCH wasn't bad. Especially not for a free lunch. Monday's (was it Monday? I'm losing track. Days don't matter too much anyhow) - whatever, that was pretty inedible. I've found leftovers in the park, for sure, that were better. Just have to be very careful about those, that's all. Observe the people, wait. Do a visual check. Get to it quick before something else does. But glad to have a few recycling dollars in my pocket, just in case.

Oops, time to move. Here comes Maggie with that hound of hers. Pit Bull. I don't care how many times she tells me and everyone else that the dog is a lover, a baby. I don't trust it. Don't like the look of its jaws and don't believe it is free from, what, thousands of years of history and genes. Besides, Maggie's crazy. There are times she's just plain out of control, and it's good to not be anywhere near. Schizophrenia. She takes drugs sometimes. Sometimes not. Looks like this is a *not* time. Waving her arms around like a wild woman talking to the sky and the kingdom of god and angels, whatever. I bet by the end of the day she's talking with the park rangers or the cops. They're pretty nice to her. Understanding. They don't belong in jail ... the sick people. They belong someplace else. Someplace safe. For them and everybody else.

I'm not crazy.

REALLY?   Three bad shows in a row. I suppose when you have to do them everyday it's hard to get them all right. But still. Even Dr. Phil was a rerun. Maybe it is time to get that expanded channel package. But who can watch 1000 channels? I'm having a hard time with 600!

"Jasper, do you want mommy to get you the Animal Channel? Would that make my big boy wag is little tail?"

Lunch, lunch. Boring, boring. But the croissant wore off. Weight Watchers frozen lemon chicken? Doesn't matter. Fuel units. Check the mail. "Jasper, Jasper, come with mommy. Guard the door. Good Boy!"

Magazine, bills, junk, junk ... I already joined AARP, thank you! Another set of stickers from the ASPCA. Didn't I just send them money? Gawd, I wish they would not send those things and make me feel guilty!

The guys are back in the park. Wonder if they'll start

drinking. I'll call the ranger for sure this time. Why can't they go somewhere else? Homeless, but money for beer.

Lemon chicken and broccoli, 2 minutes, 30 seconds. Readers Digest or Redbook? Too many young people in there to be interesting. Oprah this afternoon. Hope it's not a rerun. Of course, it's a rerun. Oh well. "Does Jasper want one little piece of mommy's chicken? Yum, yum!"

NICE sunset. If the almond factory wasn't in the way, you could really see it. But, anyway, the light on the building actually looks pretty. A lot prettier than what happens inside, so far as I am concerned. Women with their hair all tied up in nets. Coming outdoors for, what, a 15-minute break and then shuffling back inside for a few more hours of fillin' cans, putting labels on … Same thing over and over again.

Tomorrow should be Tuesday. Trash pickup on the west side of the street. Need to get out here early and work it before they all show up. House over there is good. A rental. Kids in their 20s. Soda cans and beer cans. That woman's place across from the park always has wine bottles. Think somebody there has a problem. I can't manage too many of those anyway. Too heavy. A few, though, is good. More money. Maybe I'll get a bike. Maybe not. Just something else to worry about getting swiped. A can crusher! Santa, will you please bring me a can crusher for Christmas this year?

Lights are coming on. She's pulling her drapes shut. Nighty night. So glad you let your little dopey dog out in the park to poop. Too bad you didn't pick it up, again! I think there's a law against that. Maybe I'll report her. Turn her in. She's always calling on us. Not me personally, cause I am very careful. But the others. Get a life!

THERE she goes. Wandering off in the direction of the shelter or the River. Don't know which. She's pretty clean. Must be the shelter. I wonder what happened to her. Probably smells bad. Most of them do. Is she sick? Doesn't look drunk. No matter. I could never live like that.

"Come on pup, come in the house. Time for our din-din. Tri tip for me, buffalo bits for you!" A nice glass of wine. Netflix. A good sappy drama. And Beddy-bye.

5.
The Morning Watch

Making it slowly up a hill in my neighborhood, my
dog Murphy urging me along, we turn a corner and look
into the distance. Up near the top, shrouded in morning
fog, are a handful of cars parked on the verge of pine nee-
dles and dirt. Near the center of the street, there is a spec-
ter, a figure of a woman standing still as the trunks of the
pines that hug the road. Many yards down the hill from
the woman I see a young girl, maybe twelve or so, walking toward me, carrying books in her arms and staring

studiously down at the pavement.

As I work my way closer, I see the woman is wearing white, perhaps a classic white robe tied at the waist. Her arms are folded across her chest in a gesture that might ward off the chill. Hugging herself as she might hug the girl walking to the school bus stop. She stands still as a statue, watching and waiting.

I remember back so many decades when I was the girl's age. By then, I'd been walking the mile or so to and from school alone for many years. Navigating the town blocks without fear of anything worse than mischievous neighborhood boys being boys. But this is a different day it seems, even in this rural place I get to live.

I am sure the girl knows that her mother is a foggy guardian on the street above her. That looking back might encourage continued protection. That she hopes none of the other bus kids witness this act of deep love, perhaps mistaking the vigilance as a lack of trust in her.

The fog has lifted some, and we pass the girl. Her head is lowered, looking at her own footfall. I wave and give her a smile. She glances up briefly and politely responds with a tiny wave back.

I hear the school bus in the distance, and the girl's

pace quickens. I know when the bus has glided to its stop because the mother turns toward her driveway, her long brown hair dancing just a bit in the breeze. I am close enough now to see her turn her head to glance one more time down the hill making sure the bright orange bus has her daughter safely onboard.

Mom sees us marching up the hill and gently smiles at Murphy and me. I am struck by the strong resemblance between her and the girl. There is very little difference, save for the years that distinguish them.

Still hugging herself in the warmth of the robe, she walks down the driveway to her home. The fog has lifted, and her own day has begun.

6.
When a Home is Not

June 2, 1978

It's been one month since I started my job as the activity director at the convalescent home. Low Pay but lots of satisfaction – along with frustration about how the patients (residents?) are cared for (or not). I'm making a real bond with some of them, especially Gracie, who follows me around most days. She's pretty much a child in the body of a middle-aged woman. No teeth (except for a pair of false teeth that she is constantly misplacing), a glass eye that stares oddly to the left, and the delightful habit of sputtering out long phrases of cuss words as she roams the halls. I suspect I am one of the few people who is actually amused by this idiosyncrasy.

There are plenty of people on the inside of these institutional green walls worth noting. And they seem to have little in common except for the fact that they've all been sentenced to live out their years in this convalescent home. However, I always thought that 'convalescing' meant resting to get better — and go home. That's certainly not in the cards for these folks. There are people with developmental disabilities, elders with dementia, folks with physical ailments that required constant care, and even youngsters with lifetime afflictions whose families can't (or won't) care for them at home.

I've been told that Gracie is a victim of fetal alcohol syndrome. The patients' charts are oddly free of details, and most of what I know about them comes from nurses' aides and younger men called orderlies who wear white coats, mostly help move people around and do clean up. I asked Head Nurse Hatcher for details and she made it clear that this is "None of (my) concern" and that I should stick to cards and bingo with the folks she calls "guests".

Anyway, Gracie and several others make the place more than bearable. It's interesting, and I feel it's kind of important to brighten up their lives with some silliness, music, and physical movement. I found I can pretty much do what I want because Nurse Hatcher only makes an appearance in the wards when someone is very sick or dead. Her time is spent in an office off the lobby of the facility where she can welcome the families of prospective patients while making sure none of the current residents' attempts to walk out the front door.

I've been using one of the fire doors to take Gracie out because she was in desperate need of clothes to match her personality. When I first got there, she'd been dressed in baggy, colorless clothes. Cheap house dresses that camouflaged her youthful spirit. I made visits to a couple thrift shops for brighter clothes that she likes so much she sometimes double up her outfits – like wearing two skirts or blouses at the same time. She's also taken to following me around and helps to cheer up other residents. That's good because some of them are aware of becoming long forever-residents and are understandably depressed. Gracie makes people laugh. Some even enjoy her bursts of profanity that erupt without any apparent cause.

Last week she told me her favorite food was a strawberry sundae. I asked when she last had one, and she launched into a barrage of curses. So, I treated her to a sundae – we went out the emergency exit and off to Bob's Big Boy. I think she's becoming a legend there too because she showed a talent for downing the entire sundae in just a few big bites. Gracie did this by removing her false teeth and placing them on the lunch counter before attacking the sundae. I mean eating whipped cream, nuts, cherries, and all in spoonfuls the size of coffee cups. She had the whole wait staff in awe! They want me to bring her back.

June 16, 1978

I've got a new fan! Along with Gracie often trailing me around halls, I've got a buddy named Rex, who sometimes joins us (but not for long because Rex doesn't track well). He looks to be in his fifties, and his chart reported a diagnosis I was unable to find in any medical dictionary. One of the orderly guys said he drank and drugged himself into semi-consciousness. This is really on display when Rex tries to tell me (or anyone) something. He can't speak an entire sentence. He comes to me, looks me in the eye and says, "I want the …. er, ahhh….. going to a … ahh, ahhh….." Then he starts to shift from one foot to the other in a kind of nervous dance, and the thought drifts off.

I think I figured out that most of attempts at communicating mean Rex wants a cigarette, so I tell him I'll come get him when its time for the smokers' group in the Day Room. But I did learn really fast that lighting up isn't all he wants. Rex eats cigarettes. Yes, eats them. One of the nurse's aides told me that last Christmas someone (likely a guilty relative who never comes to actually visit) sent him a carton of Marlboros. She said he ate a pack and a half before they stopped him.

Many of the people I am getting to know are like Rex and Gracie, clearly challenged with mental disorders either by birth or life experience. Some are able to express themselves and interact with others. Also, there are intelligent people who suffered a physical challenge that apparently cannot be handled in a family home. I think I feel the saddest for them because they know they are living out a life sentence delivered through no fault of their own.

I've tried to cheer these folks as best I can. Jokes, books, music, listening to their stories. One woman, Brenda, is especially troubling because I think lack of attention is hastening her condition. She has Parkinson's, and her hands shake a lot. She hasn't been out of bed except to go to the bathroom since she was placed at the home, she tells me. Anyway, I went to the library and looked up that nasty disease. One thing was pretty clear – getting zero exercise does cause faster decline! I've decided I am going to walk her up and down the hall – she's got a walker in the closet. Brenda told me she used to teach elementary school and says she loves children and regrets not having any of her own.

Also, this gives me an idea. I think I will get a group of them together in the day room a few times a week and do gentle exercises while seated. With music. It will be fun!

June 29, 1978

Dear future me, when you read this, years from now, you've got to believe that no one will be treated like Anita is at this convalescent home. The notes at the end of her bed list "birth deformity" as the cause of her condition. She has a normal size head and body, but tiny legs and very short arms. Anita hasn't been out of bed since I started working at the home. She's put on her stomach and positioned so that she can see out to the hallway (I guess that was to serve as social life?). I've found that I can make her laugh, though you can hardly hear her. Same with talking – she likes to chat, but it's all in a whisper. Logically, that's because she spends so much of her waking life with her weight on her chest. She has no lung capacity for air to push out her small voice. She tells that she has not been outdoors – felt any sunshine - since she arrived at the facility. I'm going to get the orderly (the one that has a little crush on me) to get her up and in a wheelchair and into the Day Room.

July 12, 1978

Took Gracie out for ice cream again, and she's like a celebrity at Bob's! Seriously, they all come up and say hello to her, even argue about who will bring her sundae to the table. I'm also aware there have been some bets placed by the staff about how many bites it will take her to make the sundae disappear. She averages between five and three. Gracie adores the attention. She laughs with them and gets some hugs from a couple of the waitresses. One of them brought her a little cloth doll dressed up in a strawberry apron. This kind of makes up for the negative attention she got at the home last week. I wasn't there when it happened, but the aids told me – and they were trying hard to not laugh too loud. They said that Nurse

Hatcher had made one of her infrequent visits to the ward because a family member of a resident had visited (like snow in July) and heard Gracie deliver one of her profanity-laced orations as she scooted down a hallway. The visitor threatened to move her family member to another facility (which would have been a blessing for the patient, by the way). So, Nurse Hatcher shoved Gracie into her room and gave her a loud scolding – that I am told also contained some blue zingers – shut Gracie's door and locked her in for the afternoon. Let out that night after the office staff had gone home, Gracie went to the reception area to the drinking fountain next to Nurse Hatcher's office, popped out her glass eye, and put it atop the drain. I don't have to tell you who found it the next morning, do I?

My chair exercise group is going well, especially for Brenda. She still shakes, of course, but she seems able to make it down the hall with her walker more confidently. And she is smiling more and talking to some of the other women in the group. Rex also comes to the session but does his usual shuffling from side to side to participate.

The best news is that Anita has joined us. My orderly friend rolls her in, propped up to sit in a special, high-back wheelchair. She's strapped in and safe. She is all smiles and giggles and tries to follow along with her diminished appendages.

And I don't want to forget to mention another couple of special characters. The first is named Gretchen, according to her chart, but she tells me (over and over) that her stage name is Greta. She's well into her sixties and dresses herself in flowing clothes, topping off her glamorous look with a large-brimmed hat. This is her story: "I am a movie star, you see. I was in several films. Hollywood, you know. Perhaps you've seen some of my films?" Her voice is always lowered, like Lauren Bacall's throaty voice, when she tells me this story. She swishes her arm around in graceful gestures while talking, gracing me with a toothless smile. She's living in a beautiful world that defies the reality of this colorless facility. And I understand that. She comes to the exercise session and participates by standing up and gently moving her body like a dancer.

The second is a frail ninety-year-old woman named Nancy. She is from England. She sits up in her bed, wearing a modest pink nightgown with white lace along the collar and sleeves. Her bed is pushed up against the window and the light streaming through circles around her blonde curls like a halo. She is tiny, like a delicate bird and sits up straight when I visit her. She tells me the same thing in her lilting British accent every time we talk. "I am a ninety-year-old nanny," she says with a smile. "I've raised so many children, you see. So very, very many! I am a nanny!" I think I enjoy hearing this as much as she enjoys saying it. Sometimes she tells me about her 'children,' and how she does miss them and hopes to see them again soon. She's every bit the English lady – polite, not a complaint, because that would be rude. Brimming with memories mostly left behind in a homeland she misses and will never again visit. She lets me hold her hand. It feels like fragile porcelain.

August 6, 1978

Before I write about the most important thing that happened today, I want to make sure I mention two people who have bolstered my belief in the power of friendship. They are an unlikely pair. Georges is an elder man of Greek heritage confined to his wheelchair and Tyke, a boy of about ten-years-old, also in a small wheelchair. Tyke, I was told, had fallen into a swimming pool and 'drowned' before being revived, leaving him with an oxygen-starved brain. He cannot talk and appears to have no response to the outside world.

Georges seeks out Tyke each morning and pushes the boy along in front of him, steering his own chair with one hand. Georges's English isn't great, so he talks softly to Tyke in Greek. Tyke sometimes raises his head and looks into Georges's eyes as if he understands, though the staff swears he has no conscious reactions. The pair rolls into the community room, down the halls and to one of a few places that has a small window looking out on a world neither of them will ever experience again. Georges has been teaching me a few Greek words, Yassou! Kalimera!

August 15, 1978

So, I may need that second language because I had an unplanned encounter with Nurse Ratchet (aka Hatcher). The Dark Angel in a white cap. Florence Nightingale from Hell. It has become routine for me to sneak Anita outdoors once a week … out a locked patio door on the back of the building. Again, my orderly friend who feels compassion for Anita and a misguided passion for me, lets us out and pulls shut the curtains that cover the door. Anita just glows with the prospect of fresh air. Only to-day, Nurse Hatcher was conducting a tour for a prospective family wanting to abandon their disabled family member. And when Broomhilda grandly swept open the curtains to display the never-used patio to her potential clients, there we were, enjoying sunshine, dead grass and weeds (though some of the weeds had nice flowers). I heard her muffled voice telling the family how the patio was undergoing landscaping with a garden planned and seating – yada yada ... And the look Nurse Hatcher shot at me as she closed the curtains could have killed the weeds. I am called to her office for a meeting in the morning.

I can't say I am surprised. I've been working on borrowed time almost since the first day I got there.

September 6, 1978

This will not be the first time I've been called into the Head Nurse's office. I'd previously made the mistake of trying to appeal to her on some issues, including the need for physical movement and fresh air for patients. But she was formidable and lectured me about liability and lawsuits; how vulnerable 'her' patients were. There was no warmth or compassion in her steel-colored eyes when she instructed me about limits and responsibilities. She informed me that I'd already been seen providing services outside the scope of my position. That I needed to pop into rooms, say a friendly hello, play a game of cards in the community room, and stick to that. Most pointedly, she mentioned I'd been seen escorting Brenda along the halls with her walker. Head Nurse Hatcher explained to me that this was very dangerous.

"She falls, and you know who's liable?" she said. "I won't have that!"

I tried to counter, telling her that the literature says that exercise is very important to slow the progression of Parkinson's.

Nurse Hatcher stood up. Her face colored up like an almost ripe tomato. "Now you are a nurse? A doctor? Where's your credential? Mine's on the wall right there!" she said and pointed to her framed certificate.

I already knew my days at the job were numbered. But this encounter just cemented my determination to do as much as I could in the time had left. I was also surprised that she hadn't chastised me about my many other transgressions and had a sudden realization. Most of the floor staff had said nothing about my underground activities to her, like the chair exercise group in the Day Room or getting Anita dressed and off her tummy and out of her room, or taking Gracie with me on rounds so she could make others laugh, or dressing Gretta in new/old big hats I'd gotten at the Salvation Army thrift store.

Nurse Hatcher would only know these things if she regularly went into the wards.

That following week I kept my head down as I went through the swinging doors to the patients' rooms. I brought in new bags of clothes for Gracie and spent individual time with the people I care a lot for.

I suppose it's a little odd that the residents don't depress me. I just try to focus on who they are and what they want to say. They're an accidental community of people tossed together by fate—like a grab bag of treasure and tragedy. One thing—our relationships are totally honest. Can't say the same about lots of others outside those halls.

Anyway, today, that all came to a screeching halt because my personal vision of the Wicked Witch of the West told me I was fired.

I wish that I could have left that place with physical evidence of neglect and abuse. But alas, one thing the Hatchet Head was vigilant about was cleanliness and order. How do you document a lack of empathy and compassion?

I'd already started saying goodbye to my patients. I hate the idea of just disappearing from their lives in this abrupt manner. I will miss them a lot. But I've compiled many notes about the deficits of the place – the promises made to trusting family members and never kept. The lack of stimulation for patients. The lock-down policy and absence of actual 'care' – as in 'we care about your feelings, your health, your limited future.' When the time is right, I'll send it to whoever might have an interest in righting a wrong - a state senator, a health reporter at the local newspaper, a regulatory agency. I do believe there's payback in this unfair world. At least I want to believe that. I guess time will tell...

Anyway, here ends the entry on this part of my roller coaster ride.

June 18, 1985

Writing a postscript so many years later because I celebrate happy endings. Woke up this morning to a front-page, below-the-fold headline in the *Los Angeles Times*. The corporate chain of facilities owning the inaptly named "home" has been indicted for its practices. Neglect, license violations, misuse of medications and a string of allegations I'd be happy to corroborate and add items.

Executives will be grilled, and grievances aired by

those harmed by the multistate operation. I've already gathered up my dated, type-written notes and sent them on to some of the authorities mentioned in the story. I know this is too little, too late for my friends who languished at a home that never was. My previous attempts got no attention. Maybe the time is right?

I want to believe the investigation will shine a light, inspire more scrutiny of places in which vulnerable humans are subjected to people whose greed supplants empathy. (The Pollyanna in me is irrepressible).

I'm hoping the regulators contact me. Along with my vented-up anger, and a long list of examples of gut-wrenching neglect, I have a suggestion for the best and most instructive punishment for the guilty execs — a decade inside the walls of their own institution. No sunshine, no visitors, no parole.